Stage Fright

For Theo and Tara
P.B.
For my Dad
C.H.

Library of Congress Cataloging-in-Publication Data

Bently, Peter, 1960-
Stage fright / by Peter Bently ; illustrated by Chris Harrison.
p. cm.—(Vampire school)
Summary: When Miss Gargoyle's class stages "Snow Fright and
the Seven Dwarfs" and the lead actress loses her voice, young
vampires Lee, Bella, and Billy concoct a plan to save the day.
ISBN 978-0-8075-8468-2 (hardcover)
ISBN 978-0-8075-8469-9 (pbk.)
[1. Theater—Fiction. 2. Schools—Fiction. 3. Vampires—Fiction.]
I.Harrison, Chris, ill. II. Title.
PZ7.B4475424St 2012
[Fic]—dc23
2011035219

Based on an original idea by Chris Harrison.
Text copyright © 2010 Peter Bently.
Illustrations copyright © 2010 Chris Harrison.
Published in 2012 by Albert Whitman & Company.

10 9 8 7 6 5 4 3 2 1 ML 16 15 14 13 12

For more information about Albert Whitman & Company,
visit our web site at www.albertwhitman.com.

VAMPIRE SCHOOL

Stage Fright

Written by **Peter Bently**

Illustrated by **Chris Harrison**

Albert Whitman & Company
Chicago, Illinois

Contents

Chapter 1
Ghoul Show

The school clock was striking
nine when a small bat zoomed
up to the main entrance of St.
Orlok's Elementary School.
The bat hovered in front of the
doors for a moment, then with
a *POP!* it turned into a boy. It
was Lee Price, and he was late
for school. Vampire school.

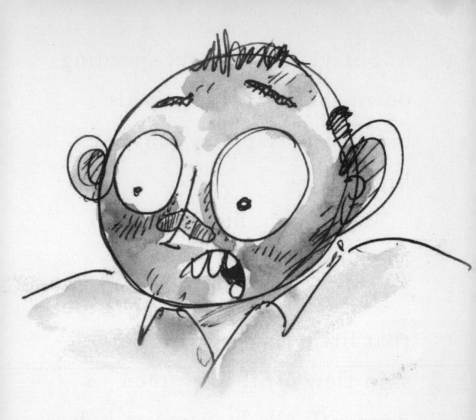

Lee dashed through the doors—and almost crashed right into Mr. E. Gore, the school janitor.

"Hey! Votch vere you're going!" grumbled Mr. Gore.

"Sorry!" called Lee, speeding down the corridor with his black cape flapping behind him.

"Late again, huh?" yelled Mr. Gore.

He shook his fist so hard that little flakes of rotten skin flew off it like green dandruff. "Pesky vampire kids! So unreliable! Ve zombies are alvays dead on time!"

Lee reached his classroom and burst in just as his teacher, Miss Gargoyle, was taking roll call. All the other young vampires turned to stare at him.

"Sorry I'm late, miss!" he gasped breathlessly, plonking himself down at a table next to his friends Billy Pratt and Bella Williams.

"Really, Lee," sighed Miss Gargoyle. She peered at the clock. "I nearly marked you absent. Tonight of all nights!"

"Sorry, Miss. I forgot my costume and had to go back home for it."

"Good grief!" panicked Miss Gargoyle. "Has anyone else forgotten their phantomime costume?"

Snow Fright
and the
Seven Dwarfs

"No, Miss Gargoyle!" chorused the class.

"Thank goodness for that," said Miss Gargoyle with relief. "There's enough to think about as it is!"

Later that night, Miss Gargoyle's class was performing *Snow Fright and the Seven Dwarfs* in the school hall. Lee had the part of Gnashful, the dwarf who was always angry.

"Mith Gargoyle! Mith Gargoyle!" piped up Lucy West, who was going to be the Wicked Queen. "My cothtume is bound to be the betht. Shall

I show it to the clath?"

"Typical West the Pest," whispered Bella. "Any excuse to show off!" Bella was playing Princess Snow Fright.

"I know," agreed Lee.

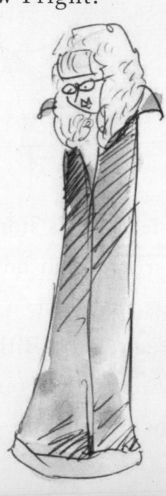

"At least she's stopped boasting about how many fangs she's lost."

"Yeah," said Billy, who was playing the hunter who took Snow Fright into the forest.

"And about how the Fang Fairy gives her two dollars for each fang."

Lucy scowled at them and stuck her tongue out.

"We'll see all the costumes after break, when we have

our dress rehearsal," said Miss Gargoyle firmly. "Until then, it's lessons as usual."

"Aw, miss!" groaned the class.

"Quiet, please, everyone!" said Miss Gargoyle. "Today we are going to practice the Three *S*s. Does anyone know what that stands for?"

"What about scaring, staring, and startling?" suggested Bella.

"Or shrieking, screaming, and screeching?" said Big Herb, secretly popping three candies into his mouth when he thought Miss Gargoyle wasn't looking.

"More like scoffing, slurping, and stuffing your face," chuckled Lee. Nobody had been surprised when Miss Gargoyle had chosen Herb to play Chompy, the greediest of the Seven Dwarfs.

"Good guesses," said Miss

Gargoyle, neatly swiping Big Herb's hidden stash of candies. "But to begin with, let's all turn into bats."

Everyone said the words that Miss Gargoyle had taught them:

"I'm a bat, a bat is me.
A bat is all I want to be."

And with a volley of soft *POP*s, they all became bats, fluttering merrily around the classroom.

Big Herb managed it on his second try. The first time

around, his mouth was so
full of candy that he said *mat*
instead of *bat* and turned into
a flying carpet.

"Now, listen and watch
carefully," squeaked Miss

Gargoyle, who was now a little brown bat. "The first two *S*s are swooping and swerving."

Miss Gargoyle swooped and swerved all around the room,

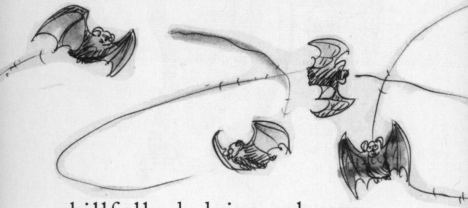

skillfully dodging columns, walls, desks, and other bats.

"Wow!" said Lee. "Cool! Wait till I show Boris!" Lee's friend Boris was a real bat who lived in the school clock tower.

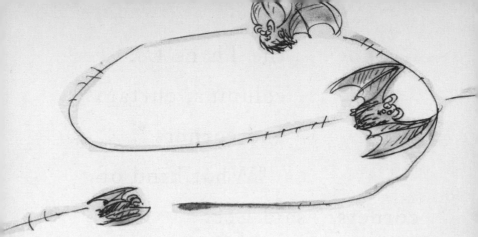

Miss Gargoyle hovered in midair to get her breath back.

"The third *S*," she went on, "is skulking. This is particularly handy when you need to turn into a bat—or back into a vampire—without any Fangless folk seeing you. When you need a place to skulk, my tip is to remember

the Three *C*s:
columns, curtains,
and corners."

"What kind of
corners?" said Lee.

"Three-*D* ones are best," said
Miss Gargoyle.

"What?" asked Billy. "As in

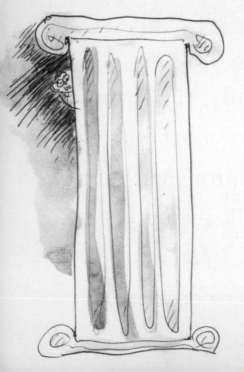

a 3-D movie?"

"No," said Miss Gargoyle. "As in dark, damp, and dingy. Okay class, now you all have a try."

They practiced the three *S*s until the bell rang for break.

"Well done, everybody," said Miss Gargoyle. "That's the end of our lessons for today. See you after break in the school hall for the dress rehearsal." She glanced over at Lee. "And don't forget your costumes!"

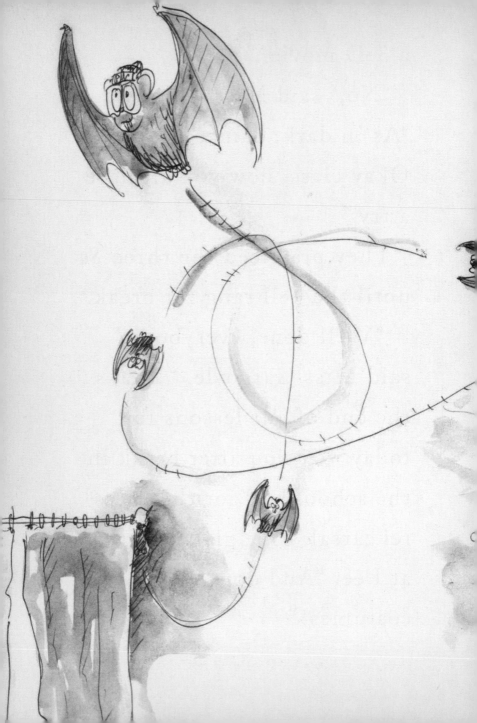

Chapter 2
First Night Nerves

During break, Lee, Bella, and Billy sat together. Lee gobbled up a packet of Drac's Snacks, but Billy and Bella ate hardly anything at all.

"I—I can't eat," quivered Billy. "I'm so nervous about this stupid phantomime. I dunno why I said I'd be in it. I hate acting!"

"You'll be fine," said Lee.

"The hunter hasn't got much to say, not like—"

"ATCHOO!"

Bella sneezed so loudly that Lee dropped his snack and Billy almost jumped out of his seat.

"Yikes, Bella!" said Lee.

"That was loud enough to wake up a zombie!"

"Sorry," said Bella. "I've got a little cold. I don't think I should have done so much skulking during the last lesson."

"Well, you did manage to find the darkest and dampest corner," said Billy. "It took us forever to find you."

"My throat feels funny, too," said Bella.

"You're probably just nervous," said Lee. "After all,

you have the biggest part."

"And you have to sing those songs all by yourself," Billy chipped in. Miss Gargoyle had asked Bella to play Snow Fright because she had the best voice in the class.

"Yeah," said Lee. "In front of the whole school."

"And lots of parents and friends," said Billy.

"Oh thanks, guys!" groaned Bella. "You've really cheered me up!"

Lee hastily changed the subject.

"Miss Gargoyle said there's going to be a special mystery guest," he said. "I wonder who it is."

"No idea," said Billy. "Didn't she say the mayor is coming? Maybe it's him."

"Oh, durrr!" snorted Bella.

"The whole point of a mystery guest is that you don't know who it is, silly."

"All right," said Billy. "Keep your cape on!"

"It's no good," said Bella. "I just can't eat. Does anyone want my snack?"

Big Herb was at the next table. Hearing the offer of free food, he whizzed around like a tornado.

"I'll have it!" he said through a huge mouthful of black pudding sandwich, some of which sprayed out onto his shirt. Then he looked at Bella's tub of beetroot salad and shook his head. "Yurggh! Actually, no thanks Bella. I forgot you're a vegetarian."

Chapter 3
Snow Fright in a Flap

After break, Lee, Bella,
and Billy went straight to the
hall and changed into their
phantomime costumes.

"OK, seven dwarfs," said
Miss Gargoyle. "Let's run

through the "Work Song" one last time."

Lee and the six other vampire dwarfs all marched across the stage in a line. They were Gappy, Snappy, Flappy, Creepy, Chompy, Gnashful, and Shock.

As they marched, they sang—

"POP-POP! POP-POP!
We'll work until we stop!
We're a scary sight,
but we won't bite!
POP-POP! POP-POP!"

On the final *POP!* they all
changed into bats and fluttered
off into the wings.

"POP!" *"POP!"*

"POP!"

"POP!"

"Excellent!" said Miss
Gargoyle. "Now, let's hear
Snow Fright's song."

Bella stood up and opened
her mouth.

"Someday my count will—
URK!"

She coughed and started again.

"Someday—URK!" Bella spluttered to a halt. "I can't do it!" she croaked faintly. "I've lost my voice!"

"Oh dear!" said Miss Gargoyle anxiously. "What are we going to do? We can't do *Snow Fright and the Seven Dwarfs* without Snow Fright!"

"Perhaps someone else could be Snow Fright?" suggested Lee.

Lucy West stepped forward.

"I'll do it, Mith Gargoyle!" she said. "I've memorized all the wordth. And I can thing much better than Bella any day," she bragged.

Bella glared at Lucy, but Miss Gargoyle said, "Sorry, Lucy. If you play Snow Fright, we'll just need someone else to play the Wicked Queen. We'll be back where we started."

"And no one could be a better Wicked Queen than you, Lucy," said Lee innocently. "You're perfect for the part!"

He winked at Bella as Lucy stomped off with her nose in the air.

"What we need," said Miss Gargoyle, "is someone who can sing but doesn't have a very big part."

"But it's too late for anyone else to learn the words!" rasped Bella. "Oh, the phantomime is going to be ruined, and it's all my fault. I'm so sorry!"

"Hang on," said Lee. "I've got an idea . . ."

Chapter 4
The Show Must Go On

The show began at three o'clock. At a quarter to three, Lee's mom and dad arrived backstage with his friend Ollie Talbot, who went to Chaney Street School for young werewolves.

"Hi, Ollie," said Lee, who was now dressed as a vampire

dwarf, with a short green cape, pointy red hat, and a fake red beard.

"Hi, Lee," said Ollie. "Cool costume! You should wear that to school every day."

"Ha-ha, very funny," said Lee. "This beard itches like crazy! I hate having hair all over my face."

"Oh, you get used to it," grinned Ollie.

"Good luck, Lee," said Dad cheerfully. "Seeing you on stage takes me back to my days with the Bat City Strollers. Did I ever play you our recording of "Fang-A-Lang"? It got to number ninety-eight in 1979."

"Yes, Dad," sighed Lee. "Only about a million times."

"Gimme a break!" came Billy's voice behind them. They turned to see Billy, dressed as the hunter, struggling to untangle his bow from the folds of Snow Fright's cape.

"Don't pull so hard," said Bella. "You'll tear it!"

Billy finally yanked the bow free.

"It's bad enough trying to remember my lines without having to carry this stupid bow," he moaned. "It just gets in the way!"

"Just relax," said Lee. "You'll be fine. You're only on in the first scene."

Lee's mom looked at her watch.

"It's five to three!" she said. "We'd better get back to our seats. The hall's almost full. All the parents have come, and lots of friends, as well as a party of werewolves from Ollie's school. I've spotted several mummies, too, and there's even a row of zombies right next to us. But I think they've fallen asleep."

"No, they haven't," said Ollie. "They always look like that."

Mom blew Lee a kiss.

"Good luck, darling. And try not to look so angry. I'm sure it'll all be fine!"

"I'm Gnashful," said Lee. "I'm meant to look angry!"

"Right," said Miss Gargoyle
after Mr. and Mrs. Price and
Ollie had taken their seats.
"It's three o'clock. Let's go for it!"
  She strode out in front of
the audience. "Good evening,

everyone! The children have
all worked really hard for
tonight's show, and we hope
you enjoy it. I have great
pleasure in presenting *Snow*

Fright and the Seven Dwarfs!"

She returned backstage and smiled at the children.

"Ready, Wicked Queen?"

"Yeth, Mith Gargoyle," simpered Lucy West. Lee, Bella, and Billy had to admit that she did look rather splendid in her Wicked Queen costume.

As the applause died down, the Wicked Queen stepped through a cardboard doorway and onto the stage. She stood in front of her magic mirror and declared:

*"Mirror, mirror
on the wall,
  Who is the fairetht
of them all?"*

The phantomime had
begun.

Chapter 5
A Screaming Success

There was one mishap
during the beginning of the
phantomime. Billy was so
nervous that he accidentally

knocked the Wicked Queen's pointy hat off with his bow. The audience found it very funny, especially when Lucy hissed, "You thtupid idiot! You've methed up my hair!"

But things went smoothly after that. There were no more mess-ups and no one forgot their lines. Even Bella appeared to have found her voice again when she came on as Princess Snow Fright. She was a little husky and faint when she spoke, but she sang as sweetly as anything:

"*One day my count will come.*
He has sharp fangs, he's not so dumb.
To his creepy castle I'll ride
by my spooky sweetheart's side."

"That was lovely," whispered Lee's mom.

"Yes," agreed Mr. Price. "But I thought all the dwarfs were in this scene? There are only six of them."

"You're right," said Mrs. Price. "Where's Lee?"

It was true. Gappy, Snappy, Flappy, Creepy, Chompy, and Shock were all sitting in their cottage around the fire—but Gnashful was nowhere to be seen.

Lee reappeared in the next scene, when the dwarfs flew home as bats and changed back

into vampires—only to find
Snow Fright in a faint from
the Wicked Queen's poisoned
apple.

But after Count Alarming
had saved Snow Fright, Lee
vanished again just before she
sang her song for the last time.

"Look!" whispered Ollie to
Lee's mom. "He's behind that
tree."

"Which one?" whispered
Mrs. Price.

"The blue one," said Ollie.
"Next to Snow Fright."

Ollie was right. After Bella's song, Mrs. Price spotted Lee slipping out from behind the tree to join the other dwarfs. He was just in time to watch the Wicked Queen scream in fury—Lucy was very good at screaming—and disappear in a puff of smoke.

"And that," chorused the
dwarfs, "was the end of the
Wicked Queen. And Snow
Fright and Count Alarming
lived snappily ever after."

The children all took a bow
amid cheers and clapping. Ollie
and the other werewolves bayed
and howled, and the mummies

flapped and waved their
bandages. The phantomime
had been a terrific success.

Mr. and Mrs. Price and Ollie
left their seats to go backstage
and congratulate Lee.

"Excuse us," said Mr. Price
as they pushed along the row
of zombies. The zombies were
the only ones not applauding
wildly.

They sat in total silence, staring blankly at the stage. As Ollie went past, one of them turned to his wife.

"Mildred, my dear," muttered the zombie. "When does the show start?"

Chapter 6
The Mystery Guest

"Well done, Lee!" beamed Mr. and Mrs. Price when Lee had changed back into his normal vampire clothes. "You were great!"

"Yeah," said Ollie. "That was a scream."

"Thanks," smiled Lee.

"Just one thing, Lee," said Dad. "Why did you keep

hiding during Snow Fright's songs?"

"Yes dear," said Mom. "Didn't you like Bella's singing? We thought she sang beautifully."

Lee grinned.

"Thanks Mom! I mean, er . . . it's kind of a long story. I'll explain on the way home."

Billy came over with his mom and dad.

"Phew!" said Billy. "I'm glad that's finished. I'd rather do math any day!"

"But you did really well,"
said Mr. Price. "We loved
that part where you knocked
off the Wicked Queen's hat.
Brilliant comedic timing!"

"It wathn't meant to be
funny!" came a familiar voice.
"Billy totally thpoilt my hair."
Accompanied by her mother,
Lucy West stomped past them
with her nose in the air and a
furious look on her face.

"Please don't fret, my precious Lucy," said her mom. "Why doesn't Mommy buy you a present to cheer you up?"

"That's right, you will!" snorted Lucy. "I want a new houthe for all my Tranthylvanian Families!"

"Yes, precious."

"And a complete thet of My Little Zombies!" said Lucy.

"Yes, precious."

"The really big ones, not the thtupid little ones!"

"Of course, precious," said her mom meekly. "Anything you say."

"Good gracious, it's not just her hair that's spoiled!" said Mrs. Pratt as Lucy marched her mother out of the hall. They all laughed, though they had to agree that Lucy had actually been really good as the Wicked Queen.

But the best praise of all was for Bella. As soon as they saw her, Lee and the others gave her a great cheer.

"Darling, that was amazing,"

gushed Bella's mom, giving her a hug. "Especially since you weren't feeling too well this morning."

"Yes," said her dad. "Your singing was fabulous."

"Er, well—" croaked Bella, but just then, Miss Gargoyle came over with a very tall vampire wearing a smart suit and an elegant velvet cape.

"This is our special mystery guest," said Miss Gargoyle. "Mr. Harker Winegum, the owner of the Horrordrome."

"What?" blurted out Lee. "The big vampire theater in town?"

"The very same," smiled Mr.
Winegum. "Now, where is
Bella Williams?"

"Here," said Bella huskily.

"Delighted to meet you,
Bella," said Mr. Winegum
with a gracious bow. "This
summer, I am putting on

The Sound of Screaming. There are seven vampire children in it. After hearing you tonight, I would like to offer you a part in the show—if your parents agree."

"Oh Bella!" squealed her mom in delight.

"Fangtastic!" said her dad.

But Bella wasn't smiling.

"That's really nice, Mr. Winegum," she

croaked. "But—but it wasn't me singing tonight."

"Don't be silly, Bella," said Mrs. Price. "We all heard you. You were wonderful."

Bella shook her head glumly.

"No. It wasn't me. I lost my voice in the rehearsal. I could just about manage to speak,

but I couldn't sing a note. My songs were sung by—Lee!"

All eyes turned to Lee. There were gasps of astonishment.

"It's true," admitted Miss Gargoyle. "Every time Snow Fright had to sing a song, Lee hid out of sight and sang it for her."

"So that's why Gnashful kept disappearing!" said Ollie.

"Yes," said Lee. "I had the words on a piece of paper. We just had to make sure Bella was always in front of a tree or

a door or something else for me
to hide behind."

"All I did was mouth the
words," said Bella.

"It was Lee's idea," said Miss
Gargoyle. "When Bella lost her
voice, it was the only way the
show could go on!"

Mr. Winegum stood quietly

for a moment.
"Of course
this means I
shall have to
change my
offer,"
he said.
Bella
nodded sadly.
"Lee deserves
it, not me," she said.
"Never mind, darling,"
her mother comforted her.
Mr. Winegum laughed kindly.
"No, no! You misunderstand

me," he said. "I would like to offer a part in *The Sound of Screaming* to Lee *and* Bella."

"What?" cried Bella. "Really?"

"The boys and girls in the show have to act as well as sing," said Mr. Winegum. "I haven't heard you sing yet, Bella, but I do know you can act. What do you say?"

"Yippee!" cried Bella.

"Hooray!" cried Lee.

"Excellent!" smiled Mr. Winegum. "We'll figure out the details tomorrow. Good evening!"

And with an elegant swish of his velvet cloak, Harker Winegum turned—*POP!*—

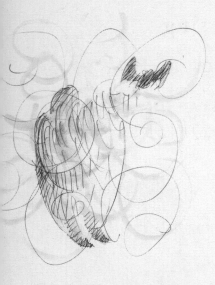

into a bat and fluttered off.

"I can't believe we're going to be in a big show!" rasped Bella.

"Yeah, that's so cool!" said Lee.

"Hey," said Billy. "Can you get free tickets for friends?"

"Including werewolves?" said Ollie.

"You bet," said Lee. "And I'll get loads of money to buy ice cream and games and . . . and . . ."

"And you'll put most of it in a bank until you're older," said Mrs. Price wisely.

"And you'll still have to go to school, you know," said Mr. Price.

"Aw," said Lee. "That doesn't

sound like much fun."

"Oh, don't worry," grinned his mom. "You'll have an incredible time."

"Let's celebrate!" said Mr. Price. "Scary Mary's I Scream Parlor is just around the corner."

"Yes, please!" cried Lee, Bella, Billy, and Ollie.

"Did someone say 'ice

cream?' "
grinned
Big Herb,
who was
just passing
by with a
chubby grown-
up vampire that
looked just like
Herb, only older.

   "OK, Herbert," said Mr. Price.
"You and your dad can come,
too."

   "Yikes," whispered Lee to Ollie.
"They'll run out of ice cream!"

When they reached Scary
Mary's, Lee paused at the
door.

"Hey," he said. "What do get
if you cross a vampire with an
ice cream?"

Everyone shook their heads.

"Frostbite!"

And to the sound of groans
and laughter, the doors of
Scary Mary's closed behind
them.

The End

Hungry for more?
Sink your teeth into the next Vampire School adventure.

These humorous chapter books are perfect for children beginning to read on their own. The young vampires' adventures will appeal to girls and boys alike.

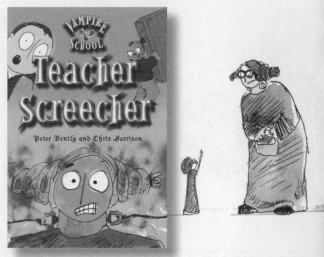

The gang is back in this fourth installment of *Vampire School*, and there's a nasty case of bat flu going around. With Miss Gargoyle off sick, the substitute teacher, Miss Fitt, quite literally turns out to be a monster, complete with neck bolts and lightning storms! Janitor Mr. Gore is up to something, but will Lee, Bella, and Billy manage to find out what?

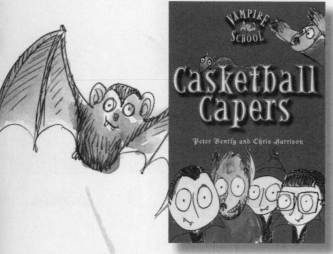

Lee, Billy, and Bella are all on the St. Orlok's casketball team. (That's the vampire version of basketball, in case you've never played it.) They're all getting ready for a big game against the Chaney Street werewolves. But when the other team arrives, it seems that some of them aren't planning on playing a fair game. Lee needs to come up with a plan—fast! Will he manage to foil the cheaters before the final whistle?

Vampire School
Ghoul Trip

Lee, Billy, and Bella and the rest of Miss Gargoyle's class are off on a school trip to the funfair. But when they arrive, there are some very strange characters hanging around. Could they have anything to do with the string of robberies that have been happening around town? Lee, Billy, and Bella decide to do some investigation and get to the bottom of the mystery.